W9-AAW-103

Mr. Meredith and the Truly Remarkable Stone

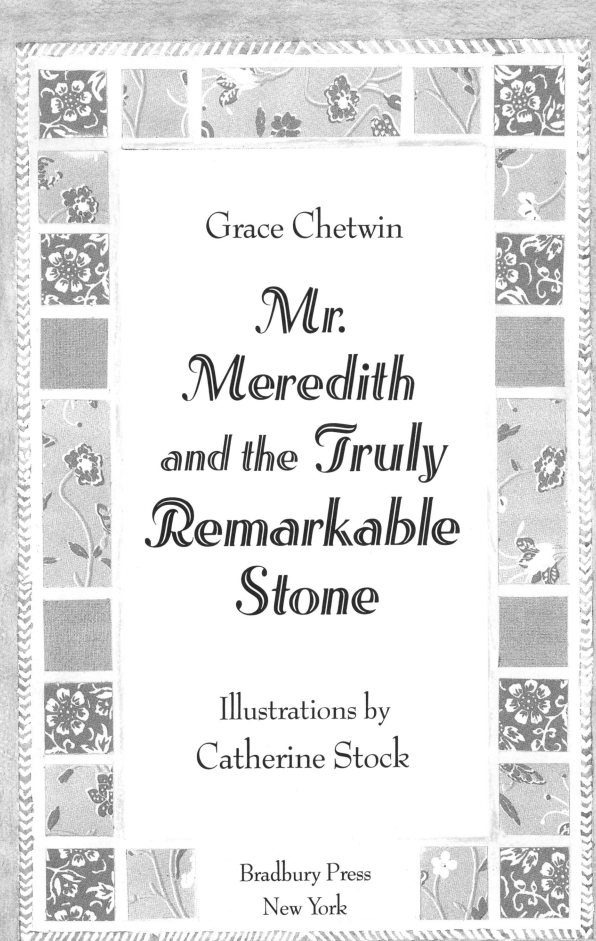

Grace Chetwin

Mr. Meredith and the Truly Remarkable Stone

Illustrations by
Catherine Stock

Bradbury Press
New York

Text copyright © 1989 by Grace Chetwin
Illustrations copyright © 1989 by Catherine Stock

All rights reserved. No part of this book may be reproduced or transmitted in any form or
by any means, electronic or mechanical, including photocopying, recording, or by any
information storage and retrieval system, without permission in writing from the Publisher.

Bradbury Press
An Affiliate of Macmillan, Inc.
866 Third Avenue, New York, NY 10022
Collier Macmillan Canada, Inc.
Printed and bound in Japan
10 9 8 7 6 5 4 3 2 1

The text of this book is set in 16 point Bernhard Modern. The illustrations are reproduced
from multimedia pieces. The artist first painted the pictures with watercolor. She then added
colored pencil, gouache, pastels, and, in some cases, collage, to complete the scenes.

Library of Congress Cataloging-in-Publication Data
Chetwin, Grace.   Mr. Meredith and the truly remarkable stone.   Summary: When
Mr. Meredith finds a remarkable stone, he builds a series of ever grander structures
in which to house it.   [1. Rocks—Fiction]   I. Stock, Catherine, ill.   II. Title.
PZ7.C42555Mr 1989 [E] 87-37435 ISBN 0-02-718313-0

For Barbara S. Lalicki, with love
—G.C.

For John and Joan
—C.S.

One day, Mr. Meredith was out walking when he
fell over a stone. It was big as a fist; smooth, and
round, and gray, with a cracked top.

"What's this!" he cried. He bent to pick up the
stone and hurl it from him. "Gracious." He looked
at it, admiring its roundness, and its grayness, and
its crack in the top. "If this isn't a truly remarkable
stone!"

Mr. Meredith carried the stone home and set it in his greenhouse.

Then he stood back to admire the effect, and took to thinking how dingy the greenhouse was for such a truly remarkable stone.

He swept the concrete floor, and polished the panes, then he spent the rest of the day rearranging his plants all around it.

Mr. Meredith was so happy with the result that he invited eight friends in to admire it.

He served pots of tea and mounds of chocolate cookies. His friends stood around, saying what a wonderful party and what a truly remarkable stone.

Mr. Meredith was pleased.

But when they had gone, he took to thinking
how the greenhouse should be grander.

So Mr. Meredith called Mr. Mason the builder.

Mr. Mason knocked down the old greenhouse, and
built a new one, higher and wider, with big curved
panes, a shiny tiled floor, and a shiny tiled pool with
a fountain.

Mr. Meredith bought bigger plants for the new
greenhouse, a couple of tall statues to set around
the stone, and a pedestal high as a stool for it to
stand on.

Mr. Meredith was so happy with the result that he invited twenty friends in to admire it.

He served kegs of beer and mounds of potato chips. His friends stood around, saying what a wonderful party, what a wonderful new greenhouse, and what a truly remarkable stone.

Mr. Meredith was very pleased.

But when they had gone, he took to thinking
things should be grander.

So Mr. Mason knocked down the new greenhouse
and built a small pavilion, with a marble floor and
three marble fountains, and some ficus trees so that
small, bright birds could fly about overhead.

T 3691

Mr. Meredith was so happy with the result that he invited one hundred people over to admire it.

He served bottles of chablis and plates of tuna fish sandwiches. The people stood around, saying what a wonderful party and what a truly remarkable pavilion.

Mr. Meredith was very pleased indeed.

But when they had gone, he looked around the pavilion: at the fountains, and the trees, and the small, bright birds flying around overhead, and took to thinking things should be grander.

So Mr. Mason built a hall, with columns, and alcoves where folk could sit, and more pools with fountains, and more trees and birds.

Mr. Meredith was so happy with the result that he invited five hundred people in to admire it.

He served buckets of champagne, and trays of caviar, and little silver dishes of after-dinner mints. The people stood around, saying what a wonderful party and what a truly remarkable hall.

Mr. Meredith was very, very pleased.

But when they had gone, he looked around the hall: at the columns, the alcoves where folk could sit, the pools with fountains, and the trees and the birds, and took to thinking things should be grander.

So Mr. Mason built an even bigger place, so big that it even covered Mr. Meredith's house.

Mr. Meredith was so happy with the result that he invited one thousand people in to admire it, and this time they stood around all night, and never went to bed, for there was not enough room in Mr. Meredith's house to sleep one thousand people.

Mr. Meredith was very, very pleased indeed.

But when they had gone, he took to thinking things should be grander.

So Mr. Mason built a bigger place with rooms for people to stay if they wanted to, and a dining room for them to eat in, anything they wanted.

And Mr. Meredith hired cooks and serving folk, and chambermaids and porters and valets and gardeners and busboys and cleaners, and soon his place was crammed with people from all over the world.

So Mr. Meredith had Mr. Mason add another wing, then another, until it took an hour to walk from end to end. Mr. Meredith put in more pools and fountains and trees and birds and places to sit and eat and rooms to sleep in.

Mr. Meredith was now so occupied that he did all his walking indoors.

One day, he was passing through an old part of the place when he fell over a stone. It was big as a fist; smooth, and round, and gray, with a cracked top.

"What's this!" he cried. He bent to pick up the stone and hurl it from him.

Mr. Meredith looked at its roundness, its grayness, its crack in the top. "Ugh," he cried, but the instant before he threw it, he looked again. "Gracious," said Mr. Meredith. "Was this my truly remarkable stone?"

He thought of the old greenhouse, and the bigger greenhouse after it; of the pavilion, and the hall, and the wonderful place he had now, and all the people come to see his handiwork.

Mr. Meredith cupped his hands about the stone, and looked down in amazement. "Yes," he said. "My stone. How truly remarkable." Then, carrying it to his bedroom, he set the stone in the frame of his window.